A Wizard for the God in the Library

M/M Gay Fantasy Romance

J.B. Black

Love is just a matter of time.

Quismat is the god of destiny. In his library, he has everything he needs. Surrounded by books containing all that is, was, and ever would be, he has all of time at his fingertips. Nothing can surprise him.

Until a wizard appears out of nowhere.

Kenji rebels against magical theory. If the fae could create another dimension, then he could time travel.

When a spell goes wrong, he stumbles across the Library of Destiny and the god, Quismat. It's love at first sight, but breaking free of the main timeline has consequences.

A Wizard for the God in the Library *is a standalone gay fantasy fated mate romance with no cheating, no cliffhangers, and a guaranteed HEA.*

Other Works By JB Black:

Nobility Fated Mates Novellas
The Fae King's Fated Mate
The Fae Prince's Fated Mate
The Fae Lord's Fated Mate
The Crown Prince's Fated Mate
The Sorcerer's Desert King
The Erlkonig's Fated Mate
The Warlock's Royal Admirer
The Warlock's Questing Prince
The Fae Prince's Unseelie King
The Warlock's Viking King
The Warlock's Royal Courtship
A Fae Prince for the Mortal King
The Warlock's Emperor

Fated Mates of Gods Novellas
The Wandering Warlock's Fated Mate
Forest God's Fertile Hunter
From Forest God's Head Scribe to Fertile Bride
The Island God's Fated Mate
The Sea God's Pirate Mate
Fated for the Harvest God
Claiming the God Below
Claiming the Sea God
Claimed by the Crossroad God

A Wizard for the God in the Library
by JB Black

Table of Contents

Chapter One

There were few bastions of magic left in the world. In some ways, Kenji believed the rise of science fiction should've inspired wizards beyond the limitations of chaos, but the Council of Magic seemed to remain ready to accept the same rules. At first, they scoffed at *Frankenstein*, laughing about how magic had necromancy and golems despite the very rules of magic forbidding the practice and doing everything to eradicate the knowledge. For all that magic users claimed to be more advanced than mortals, they burned books just as readily if they felt the knowledge was undesirable.

Kenji had no intention of respecting the limitations of his forefathers. As a student of Aelion Academy, he ignored the traditional roots, electing to throw himself into coursework on theory and horomancy, taking up a nearly defunct branch of wizardry that many thought belonged to celestial beings alone. If the chaos which served as the original and source of all magic could shift along temporal lines, then Kenji would have his time machine one day.

Since its inception, horomancy moved objects upon personal timelines. Started as an attempt to achieve immortality, it proved to be unpredictable on living objects, often resulting in anything with a complex neurological system crumbling into vegetative sludge. A magic user could move an object back and forth along its individual timeline, but from the perspective of the main timeline, the object remained firmly in place. What happened to it during and following the casting had no effect on the object's past. Food could go rotten and be brought back. Trees could be aged to fruit, but other sorts of magic worked in tandem, botany and the druidic arts needing to be applied at the same time to prevent unpredictable outcomes. An item could be fixed, sliding back along its timeline, but if torn, it couldn't be sent ahead to when it was fixed. Instead, time could only be applied as if nothing occurred to the object at all to fix it. Aging in its current state. In that way, horomancy proved an absolute waste of time for anyone but druids who only used it as a secondary approach.

Kenji Nakamura refused to accept this. He came from a long line of wizards on his father's side, and his mother was a druid from a long line of her own. Growing up, he watched his mother preserve flowers using horomancy for her flower shop and ikebana, so he knew the concepts. Frankly, even before attending Aelion Academy, he understood horomancy better than most wizards, so getting on the theoretical track wasn't too difficult. Made all the easier by his long family line, though some sneered at his father for marrying a druid.

They were idiots. Limited in their ability to understand the minutia of magic.

In his workroom, Kenji reviewed his calculations, debating again how much the planet moved within the universe and how to undermine his location when trying to move himself upon the axis of the main time stream. If current magical theory proved true, then the universe functioned on a closed loop. Which meant if he went anywhere then he was always designed to go there. That meant time travel, if possible, was generally pointless for anything but observational purposes.

While Kenji refused to believe in closed loop time, he also refused to accept it made time travel pointless. Accumulation of knowledge or retrieval of knowledge lost didn't mean the time stream had to be affected. If time existed in a closed loop and could not be changed, then nothing Kenji did could ruin the time stream; therefore, he could find those texts that the Council of Magic destroyed. He could go back in time to the creation of Faerie and learn how they had managed to construct an entire dimension with only a pair of fated mates at its foundation. Sure, now there were numerous celestials keeping the realm stable and expanding it day by day, but at its core, a two fae managed it without blessing or assistance of any sort.

Five minutes — that would be all he would try for his first attempt. He had a wall of clocks set up in the far corner and as he drew the circle, he verified his placement. Every symbol and ingredient was perfectly placed. Forward versus backward — time suggested progression would prove simpler. Swimming against the current never came as the easier option.

Adjusting his clothes, Kenji settled the enchanted breathing mask on his face, praying it would not be necessary before he gave himself to the giants of magic and science. An explosion of light came first. It was like standing in the center of a holographic display of the origins of the universe. Heat painted across his skin, but his shielding held, and from one blink to the next, the world shifted around him — light then something purer than darkness. A void stretched then another flash of light, and Kenji stumbled forward, tripping over his own feet and taking someone else to the ground with him.

"What are you doing in my workroom?" Kenji demanded before his eyes had even adjusted.

Shoving him off her, Amber — a classmate in the theory course — huffed, "You're the idiot who portaled into my workroom! What are you doing in that stupid getup?"

Kenji stood, offering a hand to help her to her feet, but Amber pointedly rejected him, standing and brushing off her own robes before returning to her own chalkboard. Baffled, Kenji cursed at the broken watch on his wrist.

"What time do you have?"

"Three after one," Amber grumbled, glaring at him. "What were you even trying to do? You're ice cold!"

He couldn't exactly admit his intentions to someone who saw him as a rival. Either the professors would think he was insane, or they would consider him dangerous. Perhaps even both. Until he proved his hypothesis, he couldn't afford too much attention. However, when he had tried to move five minutes ahead, he found himself fifteen minutes in the past. Just enough time that he couldn't run to the other side of the castle in time to catch himself before he performed the smell. Of course, he could teleport, but even calling upon his magic left his head spinning. Teleporting right now would make him a danger to himself twice over.

That was when he noted the calculations on Amber's chalkboard. He wasn't the only one not actually researching what he claimed to the department head.

"Oh, now that is interesting," Kenji laughed. "Let's call this an agreement of silence."

Amber glared at him. "Shut up."

"My lips are sealed," Kenji promised, miming zipping his mouth shut before continuing,

"Now, we have no proof the Realm of Destiny exists."

Blue eyes narrowing, Amber scoffed, "If Death and Love can have gods, then Destiny can as well."

"I'm not arguing that, but where the Underworld exists as a realm, Love doesn't have one," Kenji retorted, running a hand through his dark hair as he lowered his mask to hand about his neck. "Even if it did, your equation using Kepler's Constant when we have no reason to believe Destiny wouldn't reside in a side realm like the Underworld with portals in multiple realms."

"If I were trying to locate the realm itself and not a doorway into the realm, then perhaps you'd be right, but I'm looking for an entryway which resides in our realm, so Kepler's Constant is right," Amber retorted curtly. Crossing her arms over her chest, she demanded, "Get out!"

"Isn't this more seer babble?"

Amber glared, storming past him to add another symbol to the runic circle around the door she'd constructed. There was no actual door, so it was really just a frame where one might appear. It frankly looked a bit bizarre, but a cursory glance at her formula and the symbology suggested her theories were sound, and entering an unconfirmed realm with a god no one had seen or even had a name for in the annals of magical history pulled at the very core of Kenji's self-interests.

"Nakamura, either shut up or get out," Amber spat, glaring at him. Her hands trembled and shoving the chalk back a bit more violently than necessary into the holder, she shoved up her sleeves. "If you're staying, make a protection circle and actually put your magic where your annoying presence is!"

Grabbing the chalk, Kenji quickly drew a circle, crouching into a low squat and drawing lines between them. He had no intention of intervening directly, but he could lend her the limited remains of his magic. One of them ought to get something out of this day, and while moving backwards in time supported his hypothesis, it also showed his calculation was significantly off. A multitude of three beyond his goal and in the opposite direction as well as on the other side of the castle — he had some major corrections to make.

Kenji expected to feel faint. To have his magic drawn to the last drop to accomplish Amber's goal, but instead, a gust of wind swirled as the air rippled like the surface of a pond, and a door solidified in the frame. There wasn't much to it. A solid oak door with a brass handle. Nothing spectacular. Nothing beautiful or otherworldly. Even Amber stared in confusion.

"That was — that was too easy, wasn't it?" Amber asked him, but despite her uncertainty, she cast a few safety checks before crossing into the main circle and reaching for the doorknob. It turned, and an entire other world stood on the other side. "A library?"

"The Library of Destiny," Kenji whispered, coming up behind her.

A maze of shelves and books folded around upon itself before them. It was like the castle at the center of the goblin city, and though Kenji worked with science fiction more than fantasy, he adored David Bowie enough to marvel at the insanity of the maze which shifted upon itself. Vast and overflowing with knowledge.

When Amber froze on the threshold, the dark-haired wizard looped around her, trying to get a better look before asking, "Well, are you going to go in?"

Amber inhaled slowly. "This is big."

"All that is, was, and ever will be, right? Seems about the right size," Kenji told her, but she remained frozen. Lifting his mask back into place and checking the protective warding on his clothes, Kenji announced, "If you aren't going in, can you move? I'm up for an adventure."

Rolling her eyes, Amber stepped inside with Kenji right behind her. The door remained in place, but where it had stood in the center of the room without any walls before, it settled firmly between two bookshelves with a label right above the door that gave the doors exact coordinates in time and space. Right below those, it stated, "Amber's Workroom."

"That's not disturbing in the least," Amber huffed, shaking her head at the sight. "At least we'll know how to get back and which door is ours."

Glancing around, Kenji frowned. "There aren't any other doors."

"That we can see from here."

She had a point. Still, the dark brown floorboards stretched in all directions. Mazes built from bookshelves with ornate carvings upon them and books upon books to fill them. Dark and warm, the library shifted warm yellow light from nowhere at all.

When the door shut behind them with a soft click, both jumped. Kenji's heart raced in his chest — a mix of fear and excitement churned in his blood, but the door remained right where it was, and when Amber opened it again, her workshop stood on the other side.

"We should stick together," Amber murmured, but the way she glanced around, Kenji doubted she wanted him to see her exact reasons for coming here.

With a shrug, Kenji grinned. "Meet back here in thirty minutes?"

Turning her wrist, Amber sighed, showing him her watch. "Time isn't moving in here."

"Ah — and my watch is…" Kenji trailed off, frowning. His watch broke in the spell, yet here in the library, his watch almost laughed up at him when he looked to see it entirely fixed, ticking away merrily. "Weird, mine is working. I'll come find you in a half hour."

"You'll have to let me know what spell you used, so I can fix mine for next time," Amber told him even as she already wandered off, obviously looking for something very specific.

Kenji hummed, shaking his head. He hadn't cast anything unusual on it at all, and even his protective wards failed, so there was no reason for it to tell time in this realm, but he wouldn't look a gift horse in the mouth. Watching Amber head down one hall, Kenji spun upon his heels, debating his direction before allowing his feet to take him through the library, dragging his fingers along the side of the books as the whole of time and space stretched out around him.

Chapter Two

The library twisted upon itself. Up and down failed to matter as he wandered up random stairwells and across bridges that went over spinning towers of scrolls. A number of books tempted him, but Kenji found his feet leading him deeper and deeper. His own book had to be here somewhere, and if he could skip ahead a bit, then he could disprove closed loop hypothesis, see how the time stream reacted to a paradox, and have some useful foresight to smooth the way in his own life all in one go.

Dark academic glory — no windows, just dark wood and dark fabrics, creating wonderful alcoves to hide away in if only Kenji could find the book he wanted. Now and then, large walls of stone spanned between levels. Some had ladders between floors, but they were upside down starting from the top and switching to the bottom. Others had hollows for scrolls. Each one had a name upon it, dates and locations marked each. With the whole history of the universe inside, there had to be duplicates. It was a beautiful organization of chaos. Kenji loved every bit of it.

With all the information in the world, the library promised to hold every secret Kenji could ever desire, but there wasn't enough time to go through and seek them all. The key to horomancy had to be somewhere in the library, but the more Kenji explored the library, the more time seemed to shift strangely as the library moved around him every now and then.

He lost track of Amber a while back, but he spotted her on the ceiling — or perhaps he was on the ceiling — being guided down a hall that moved and shifted almost preemptively for her. Following her from above, Kenji crouched down, drawing a quick check. Time moved strangely in the library. While Kenji's watch measured time, the ambient magic in the library suggested time existed in a crunched space. Unlike Faerie, the alternate dimension of the library existed without any anchoring to the mortal realm. However, while not anchored, the existence of the books suggested there had to be some sort of tie to the timestream.

"If it's a way station outside of timeline, then it could be used like a central hub," Kenji murmured, writing out the calculations in his pocket notebook.

Until he found his own book, he couldn't disprove the closed loop hypothesis. If there was any malleability to the timeline, he couldn't be sure until he saw his book and reacted against whatever he saw; however, if he discovered that his book moved in a direction he wanted, perhaps Kenji should instead move to condense his personal timeline.

Caught in his theories, Kenji usually became blind to the world, but the usual solid backings of the bookcases shifted, and delighted that he could see right through, Kenji looked up only for his heart to skip a beat. Curled up in one of the alcoves, a pale man sat with short straight white hair. His dark eyes drifted across the book in front of him as a dark blanket curled about him. His features were as delicate as a porcelain doll. Plush lips and long pale lashes drew Kenji's gaze, leaving him stunned and nearly overwhelmed.

Always obsessed with magic, Kenji never thought about anything else. His whole world revolved around magical theory. His history only held one night stands and moments of mutual gratification. Kenji never wanted more. People were a distraction, but as he gazed through the bookshelf, the wizard forgot all about his desire to find his own book. Something pulled him toward the man. Demanded he break through the shelves or climb over them if he had to in order to meet the other man.

A caw sounded, and Kenji ducked, hiding though he had no need, and through the shelves, he watched as a crow landed, transforming into a black-haired man with feathers braided into his long dark hair.

"My lord," the crow shifter greeted. "I've brought your tea."

He bowed, setting down a teapot and a cup with a saucer. The crow shifter set an entire time low to the ground. It almost looked like a kotatsu, reminding Kenji of home. A blanket would have completed the look, but as the pale man slid down to sit at the table, it wasn't a Japanese tea ceremony served. Towers of cakes and scones settled on the table alongside the tea pot.

"I brought a second cup. Will you be meeting with our guest?" the crow shifter asked.

Shaking his head, the god of the library smiled. "I believe she will be fine on her own."

"Of course, my lord."

With a bow, the crow returned to his bird form and flew off through the shelves, but he left Kenji lamenting. Gods had mates. Red strings tethered them, forming the second they claimed their realms, which meant Kenji had no hope. He had never shown any sign of having a red string. Furthermore, if he were the god's mate, then the god would have recognized that truth from the moment Kenji stepped foot in the library.

However, if time existed outside a closed loop, then destiny could be changed, and if destiny could be changed, there was no reason for Kenji to lament as he could shift history around once he mastered horomancy and surpassed the believed limitations of the speciality. Besides, regrets came first from opportunities not taken. Kenji never met a god, and he had every intention of making the most of his remaining time in the library.

With that thought in mind, the wizard stepped back, searching for a way through the shelves, but when he couldn't see one, Kenji rolled up his sleeves, climbing the shelf and hopping down on the other side. The god didn't even look up. With his face buried in the book, the pale man reached out, patting around for his tea cup.

Kneeling beside him, Kenji moved the cup, smiling as the god took it. After taking a sip, the god hummed, flipping the page. He seemed entirely engrossed. The god seemed utterly oblivious. His focus honed in on the book, and the rest of the world floated into nonexistence. Even when Kenji took one of the scones from the tea tray, the god didn't look up. When the god set the tea back down, Kenji picked it up, taking a sip.

Up close, the god's eyes weren't just black. They were the same empty void that was sandwiched between the two bursts of light, and they drew Kenji in like two black holes. Stars and universes collided, fraying apart within that dark gaze, but snow white lashes lined those pale eyes, focusing only on the book. His lips pressed into a soft pout. When the god reached out a pale hand for the cup again, Kenji placed it back on the saucer.

The wizard shifted closer, leaning over the god's shoulder to read the book. Kenji expected some great adventurer's biography. With the whole of history at his disposal, the god had to have the best stories; however, to Kenji's surprise, the book in the god's hand wasn't anything like that at all. He read a book on the foundation of quantum physics.

"It's like you walked right out of my nerdiest fantasy," Kenji proclaimed, unable to prevent the words from slipping out.

The god startled, leaning away from him. All at once the black of his eyes shifted, spinning and shrinking until they looked almost human, but the black of the iris blended with the pupil, and as dark as they were, the whites looked too blue in comparison. Opening his mouth, the god closed it, frowning. Licking his lips, he breathed out slowly. The dart of pink left Kenji breathless. It was a flash of color against an almost entirely clean canvas of white.

Shaking his head, the god reached for his tea cup and took a sip. "You're not supposed to be here."

Chapter Three

When Quismat found his way into existence, nothing else existed. A void stretched. Everywhere and nowhere — an emptiness which remained in a state of potential possibilities. Perhaps it slept. Perhaps it simply waited, but no matter what might have been — something changed. A number of consciousnesses awoke. Quismat was among them. One of the first of a pantheon of ideals, and unlike the gods which would follow, these gods and goddesses did not get to select their realms. Instead, they were forced into situations which most found fitting. There were, of course, exceptions to the rule. Thanas enjoyed the construction of his realm, but once people started filling in the Underworld, grief overwhelmed him. Anybody with any sense would see exactly what Thanas planned, but Quismat held his tongue. Partly because he knew it was going to go horrible like it always would. Vasant came in the next generation, and he picked out spring, dancing with his flowers, and anybody with eyes knew what the spring god wanted before it ever happened, but the reality remained strained.

Of course, being the god of destiny, correctly predicting anything hardly mattered. In his realm, he had all the information in the world. All of history spanned out around him, neatly correlated after centuries of chaos. Eons passed around him.

While the gods made their realms and then watched others come forth to make their own and claim their own, the fae would grow tired of a world that didn't quite fit, and they would try their hand at the joy of creating their own realm. Every step further from the emptiness of the void fascinated Quismat, but where many gods longed for more, he found himself content with his library realm.

Quismat's library was constantly shifting. As a giant library, he had every bit of information in the universe at his fingertips. All time happened at once from Quismat's perspective — all time but his own. From his library, he could reach out with doorways to any time or place in every realm from the mortal realm to Faerie to Hell to the Underworld and beyond. His library stood as the hub between all realms — including the Nothingness.

Some considered him among the 'lonely gods.' Enki and Thanas and himself — gods trapped within their realms. It was like people forgot that everyone eventually made their way to the Underworld. Additionally, Enki had an entire city in his realm. People were strange. Quismat wasn't lonely. He had the least amount of people in his realms, but Quismat liked it that way. He had a few crow, raven, and owl shifters who served, flying through the time stream, but they often preferred to be on their own. Most of the time, they all enjoyed the quiet, but now and again, Quismat found himself irritated. When people — regardless of the realm — found themselves tormented by indecision, Quismat would open a door to his realm, letting them take a peek to gather their courage and head in the right direction. If he could help someone avoid tragedy, he would; however, there was only so much that he could open his realm without risking someone learning too much.

After so long, Quismat mastered this skill, opening a door and shifting shelves without even thinking to guide the person exactly where they needed to go to open their book at the exact page they needed to see at the exact moment, so that he could prevent them from seeing too much. As he allowed a young wizard to enter, he arranged for her doorway to stay open, sending a mental timer as he led her through the shelves toward her book.

Amber feared love. As fewer and fewer magic users had fated mates, she worried that she had no right to approach anyone. While her family expected her to marry another wizard of equal standing, she had fallen in love with the wrong sort. Another female wizard with a laugh that ended in a snort and a smile that stole Amber's attention when her parents thought she should marry a man. Terrified to break away, Amber longed for a sign that her love wouldn't blow up in her face. Love was always worth fighting for.

Grabbing a blanket, Quismat stretched and curled up into an alcove seat. He had a good book. Fiachra offered to brew some tea and fetch cakes. Frankly, Quismat was in a wonderful mood. When the tea and cake arrived, the god slipped to the lower table, curled up still as he read, sipping his tea now and then.

Lost in the foundational groundings of quantum mechanics, the god almost leapt out of his own skin when he heard an unfamiliar voice say, "It's like you walked right out of my nerdiest fantasy."

Leaning away, Quismat focused on the man, frowning at the stranger who he hadn't sensed entering his realm. Even staring at him, Quismat could see the man, but he couldn't feel him magically. The man was there and wasn't there all at once. Tan with almond shaped brown eyes and a mischievous face with broad cheekbones, the man ran a hand through his spiky black hair. It stuck where his hand left it. Dressed in black, he had a mask around his neck. He looked like some sort of futuristic assassin.

Licking his lips, Quismat shook his head and reached for his tea. "You're not supposed to be here."

"Weird, cause I'm here," the man laughed, taking the tea out of Quismat's hand to drink the rest. Pouring another cup, he took a sip before settling it back into the saucer. "I'm Kenji, by the way."

The god sighed. "I am Quismat."

"God of Destiny!"

"Yes…" Quismat trailed off. "I can get you a second tea cup."

The man tilted his head, smiling. "What? Don't you enjoy our indirect kisses?"

"I'd enjoy knowing how you got in here when you should be working on your horomancy project. In fact, I believe you're still there," Quismat noted, but where he could just reach back and find the man's book, he elected not to. Surprises were so rare. He intended to enjoy this one.

Grinning, Kenji leaned forward. "So you pay attention to my work?"

"I'm the god of destiny, Kenji Nakamura," Quismat reminded him. "I know everything."

"But not this," Kenji cockily retorted with a wink. "I ended up fifteen minutes back in time. Bit of a misstep, but it's the first step to proving my hypothesis."

Humming softly, the god took a slice of lemon cake. "If you traveled in time, what is the misstep?"

"I meant to go five mintues into the future," Kenji informed him. "Hadn't meant to move rooms either."

Brows furrowing, the god hummed softly. "How interesting — I think you removed yourself from my library."

"Did I?" Kenji's brows rose. "Well, why don't you take a glance at your own book?"

Quismat laughed, shaking his head as he closed his book and summoned a second tea cup. Pouring tea for Kenji, the god admitted, "I purposefully blind myself to my own future. When you can see all of time and space at once, surprises are rare. That's half the reason my realm is organized the way it is. Rather than continuing the multitudes in myself, I made this library. Otherwise, I'd never get the fun of a surprise."

Perhaps his penchant for enjoying the unforeseen encouraged the affection he felt, but one way or another, it hardly mattered. Quismat found the man before him intriguing. Kenji Nakamura was a talented wizard, but even as the fifteen minute gap ticked past, the cloudiness of Kenji's position in the time stream never corrected itself.

"I'm rather fond of surprises myself," Kenj laughed, grinning.

"You reject a self-consistent timeline, so I can understand that," Quismat retorted with a bright smile.

Kenji rolled his eyes with a smile, taking a sip of tea as he reached for a finger sandwich. "Don't tell me you believe time is unchangeable."

24

"I am time," the god replied. "And there are only three other individuals who would be able to function outside the timestream or alter it."

"Then there are four people who support my hypothesis that time isn't a closed loop," the wizard proclaimed, and he stretched out one leg under the low table, brushing his shoe against the god's leg.

A flare of heat rippled up the white-haired man's body. He clenched at a sudden sense of emptiness which twisted inside him, and when Quismat licked his lips, the intensity with which Kenji's eyes followed the trail of his tongue had them both swallowing and looking pointedly away.

"So, did you just follow Amber here because you stumbled across her workroom? Did you get a blessing from Felix?" Quismat asked, reaching under the table to rest his hand on Kenji's knee.

The wizard smirked. "Are you telling me there really is a god of luck?"

"Not anymore, but he gave a number of tokens away before retiring, so — I thought it might be a family thing," the god informed the younger man.

"I mean, my family is pretty lucky. That must be it because of all the things that could've gone wrong, finding my way into your library strikes me as a once in a lifetime sort of situation," Kenji joked, and he took a sip of his tea. "You know, I think the tea in your cup tastes better."

"Does it?"

Reaching out, Kenji caught the god's wrist gently and brought the cup to his lips. "Scientific theory requires verification."

"Additional data — replication of original results," Quismat agreed as their gazes remained locked. After the wizard drank, the god brought the cup back to his lip. "Well?"

"I fear my data set isn't robust enough."

Humming happily, the god murmured, "Your friend is ready to leave. I'd hate for you to get left behind."

"And I would hate to leave," Kenji admitted.

As long as he held the door, the wizard could remain, but Quismat had never felt like this before. His heart threatened to leap right out of his chest, yearning to settle into the soft curve of Kenji's smile. With every breath, they drew closer together with only the table's leg keeping them from pressing side by side to one another.

If Quismat kept the door open, Amber would likely try to take advantage of the library if he didn't send her back out as planned. Aelion Academy created students with a desperate thirst to prove themselves, and in a modern mortal world with such limited reaches of chaos, Quismat wouldn't fault Amber for trying to get an advantage for herself now that she had decided to abandon everything she knew to pursue the woman she loved. Whatever temptation pulled him closer to this strange magic user that he could not sense within his realm, Quismat had no choice but to push it aside — for now, at least.

"Well, I would hate to prevent your continued research. I'm rather invested in the results," the god announced, and with a wave of his hand, he created a gold necklace like the one he gave to those who worked within his realm. It was a delicate cold chain and upon it hung a miniature door. "Here. If you wish to return to the library, knock on the door."

Kenji took the necklace, smiling as he tapped on the gold door and heard the thundering sound reverberate throughout the library. "Thank you, Quismat."

"Consider it an investment in your experiment," the white-haired man retorted with a wave of his hand.

Catching the hand, the wizard brought it to his lips, pressing a kiss to the back. "Dream of me."

"What?" Quismat gasped.

Winking, Kenji raced off without explaining himself, and without thinking, Quismat moved the shelves to reunite the two wizards and allow them to return to Aelion Academy. The enthusiastic young man only recently turned twenty-four. There were eons between them. All his dismissiveness at Vasant's youth came back to haunt the god of destiny. No wonder Thanas hadn't expected to find his mate. Enki as well — they had given up on love, and it had come stumbling with youthful disregard into their realms.

Except Kenji wasn't his mate. Or was he? Being unable to sense him left the god ill at ease. It would be easy enough to pull up the book. To reach out and find exactly what was between them, but if there was a chance that the other was invisible because Quismat blocked his foresight from his own personal future, then he ached to enjoy the surprises which awaited him.

Chapter Four

The gold warmed him, pressing smooth against his skin, and when the doorway collapsed the moment after they passed through it with every last letter burning off the ground until it was like it had never existed at all, neither of the two wizards made any comment about any intention to try to summon another door. From the firm set of Amber's shoulders, she had found exactly what she wanted, and Kenji had the necklace — a direct doorway to Quismat.

Returning back to his own workroom, Kenji reviewed his equation, but he could find no fault, and his own excitement overwhelmed him, so he pulled out the cot he wasn't supposed to use as regularly as he did, and as he settled upon it — the last light of the setting sun stealing away the natural glow which lit the room, Kenji recalled the coolness of Quismat's skin. His dark eyes had threatened to swallow the wizard whole, and Kenji would have happily allowed himself to be consumed.

Unable to sleep, he changed into casual clothes and portaled to the nearby mortal city. He walked out in the warm spring air, enjoying studying the window shop displays. People mulled about. Some drank. Some shouted about some game or other. Their interests never collided with his own. As he mulled the error in his equation over and over again, a spot of white immediately drew his gaze, and for a second — small and stupid, he beieved Quismat would be outside his realm. His heart raced, and his stomach churned. Seeing Quismat outside his realm would mean that the other man had a mate, and as excited as Kenji would be to see him, the reality of that stirred dread inside him as well.

Luckily, it wasn't Quismat. Instead, it was a children's toy store. A snowy owl sat in the window display with a number of books, but none of them mattered. The owl reminded him of the god, and so he would have it. Of course, Aelion Academy disapproved of theft, but they hadn't caught him thus far, and he had no intention of giving himself away. Stealing the plush owl, Kenji returned to his workroom, sending out orbs of light as he tossed himself down on his cot.

"You look like an intrepid adventurer," Kenji told the plush owl. "We are going to be good friends."

Two nights of research, sleeping on his cot with the stuffed owl, Kenji repeated his experiment; however, instead of five minutes forward, he tried for only three minutes. Kissing the owl on the beak, he set the plush in the center after writing a few runes on its foot to allow him to summon it with ease if it veered off course.

As planned, the bird disappeared when he cast the spell; however, after three minutes passed, the bird hadn't returned. Sighing, Kenji turned to the summoning circle. However, he had no luck there either.

Right when Kenji prepared to give up and go after the snowy owl himself, knocking resounded in his workroom. Confused, the wizard opened the door, but nobody was there. Thank goodness. He hadn't the energy to erase the circle from the floor, and his current work was taboo. Two days without sleep left him a bit more ruined than he cared to admit, and it took an embarrassing few seconds for him to realize the knocking came from the necklace Quismat gave him. Pulling it from beneath his shirt, he set the little door upon his desk, crouching as he took the tiny doorknob between his nails and opened it.

"Did you misplace something?" a miniature version of the god of destiny asked, peeking out from the tiny doorway.

Brows furrowing, Kenji sighed, "I have, but why did he arrive in your library."

The god shrugged. "Perhaps we should continue our research."

"Our research?" Kenji repeated.

Quismat flushed a pale pink painting across the canvas of his white cheeks. "Your research, I mean."

All at once a door appeared in the room, and the tiny gold door shut as the other door opened inward. Quismat leaned against it with the snowy owl in his hand as he beckoned Kenji into the library.

"Ugh, you smell horrible," the god huffed as Kenji stepped inside. As the door closed, Quismat grabbed Kenji's hand, dragging him through the shelves. "You need a shower, and then I need an explanation."

Kenji laughed. "Feed me, and we'll see."

"Fine. You shower, and I'll prepare a meal, then you can give me a proper introduction to this fine fellow who found himself on the wrong side of creation," Quismat announced, shoving the wizard through a doorway in one of the pillars of stone.

The stone closed right behind him, but a door remained, so Kenji wasn't concerned. Trusting the god, he stripped down and stepped out into the hot springs which awaited with showers alongside the wall. It was like a darker version of the bath houses from home, and washing quickly, he sank into the hot spring with a pleased groan.

When the door opened, Kenji turned with a smile. "Are you going to join me?"

"Maybe next time," Quismat said, and with a wave of his hand, the wizard's clothes landed on a wooden stool cleaned and folded. "I'm more concerned you'll fall asleep and drown yourself here. Since I can't sense you, I wouldn't be able to sense if you were in distress."

Kenji's lips twisted into a smirk. "Oh, I am severely distressed. Join me."

"Hmm…perhaps your friend could help," Quismat retorted. He held up the snowy owl, laughing as he came to the edge of the hot spring. "He smells almost as bad as you."

Tossing the snowy owl to Kenji, the god crossed his arms over his chest. It smelt like burnt ozone. The scent itched at his nose. Frowning down at it, he reviewed the whole plush, finding places where someone had stitched it back up.

Kenji glanced up at Quismat, frowning. "Where did you find him?"

"Outside the time stream. He slipped out and couldn't manage reentry," the god informed the dark-haired man.

"Did you stitch him up?" Kenji asked.

The god nodded. "I couldn't leave him torn as he was." Shaking his head, Quismat kicked off his slippers and pulled up his pants, sitting down to dip his feet into the hot water. "I'm sure I'm not the first to say it, but you aren't a god, Kenji. If you had ended up outside of the time stream in the Nothingness, you would not have survived."

Kenji's eyes narrowed. "The Nothingness?"

"Haven't you ever wondered what exists outside of the universe?" Quismat teased with a smile.

Folding his arm on the edge of the spring, the wizard stared up at the god with keen interest. "I wasn't sure there was anything outside. But you can go there?"

"I can."

This was beyond anything the wizard had ever considered before. The god before him could step outside the time stream entirely. If something existed outside the timeline, then there was space for the timeline to shift and readjust.

"What's it like?"

Pressing his lips together, Quismat hummed, "Have you read about Eldritch Horrors?" When Kenji nodded, the god continued, "It's like that. Anyone less than a god couldn't comprehend that space and would go mad inside of it. The Nothingness is the well of chaos."

"That's brilliant!" Kenji exclaimed. It was then that it hit him. "Oh my fuck, I think I've been there."

"If you'd been there, you'd be insane or dead," Quismat retorted.

Jumping out of the bath, the wizard handed the snowy owl back to Quismat. The wizard dried himself off, dressing as he said, "It was only for a second. I saw light, then emptiness, then light, and I was in Amber's workroom."

"You concern me."

Pulling the god into his arms, Kenji smirked at the blush which spread across the other's cheeks. "Ah, you're concerned about me?"

Quismat pushed him away. "I'm concerned for your sanity."

Kenji followed the god out of the room. However, the low table caught his attention. His heart thundered in his chest. A hot pot sat on the table. It smelled just like home.

Sitting down at the table, the wizard served himself, grinning broadly. "I've been craving hot pot! It's like you read my mind!"

The god smiled. "I'm glad you approve."

As Kenji ate, Quismat shifted the shelves around them, picking out the wizard's book, but while there was something labeled for him, it wasn't a book. A piece of wood carved to look like a book sat in its place. On one side, the cover showed a doorway, and on the other, there was an hourglass. It was as if Kenji's book had petrified.

"This isn't a good sign," the god murmured, and joining the wizard at the table, he set the wood down. "Touch this for me?"

Kenji exclaimed, "Is that my book?"

"It should be."

When the wizard picked it up, pulling out his cell phone to take a picture, nothing changed. "Whoa, it's completely wood. There goes my plan to skip ahead and become the next Merlin."

"Kenji, I've never seen anything like this," Quismat told him.

Laughing, the wizard pulled Quismat closer. "Come on! I'm fine! It's just another mystery. Don't you have a sense of adventure?"

"This isn't an adventure. It's a corruption of my domain. I've existed since the beginning of the universe. I awoke before even Thanas!" the god exclaimed before he fell into the wizard's lap.

Both fell silent, staring at each other awkwardly. Before the god could retreat, Kenji shifted, wrapping his arms around him and settling Quismat more firmly in his lap. Tilting up his head, Kenji pressed their lips together. The kiss remained chaste. Just a brush of lips on lips, but a sharp shock passed through both of them like sticking a paperclip in a light socket. Jumping back, Quismat pressed a hand to his lips, but Kenji pulled the god back.

"I think we were destined to find each other," Kenji proclaimed. "My magic must've sent me off course to arrive at the right time to find Amber when you let her into the library."

Quismat's pale brow furrowed. "You're a wizard, not a sorcerer. Wanting has little to do with your magic."

"Wanting has a lot to do with you," Kenji proclaimed.

Despite the pain of their first kiss, he pulled the god into a second. Nothing changed. A shock sent them apart, rattling across Kenji's teeths. The burnt tingle might have warned others off, but the wizard laughed.

Huffing, the god grumbled, "And what would that be a sign of?"

"That was definitely more powerful than fireworks, so I'd say it's a pretty powerful sign," Kenji retorted with a cheeky grin.

"If you were my mate, I would be able to sense you," Quismat informed him before admitting, "I think."

Kenji's brows rose. "You think?"

"I block out my own future to not go utterly insane myself. Can you imagine how exhausting knowing everything that is, was, and ever will be can end up being?" the god asked, seemingly settling on Kenji's lap which only served to tighten the heat in the wizard's core.

"So I could be your mate?" Kenji posited.

Quismat sighed. "You feel like a void to me, but when I sensed the magic around that snowy owl toy of yours…it made me feel things."

"Things?" Kenji nipped at the god's neck. "What sort of things?"

"Your magic left me breathless," Quismat confessed.

His words fell between them. They were almost too large, but as the god pulled back, they turned to the food on the table, setting aside the conundrum of the wooden book and the way their kisses burned. They talked about nothing and everything. When the god finally sent him back, reminding him not to continue his research.

Picking up the snowy owl plush, the wizard gave it to the god. "Keep him safe for me!" Kenji laughed, pulling the god into another electric kiss. "I might just become a masochist at this rate."

Chapter Five

Even after Kenji left, the buzz of their kiss tingled on Quismat's lips. Unlike the rest of the so-called lonely gods, he had never cared about when his fated mate would arrive. They would find their way to him eventually, and he had plenty to keep him entertained in the meantime. However, teh static discharge of their kiss almost burned his lips. If Kenji were his mate, Quismat should've been able to sense him. His realm would've reacted to Kenji's presence.

The answer seemed simple. He could drop the fog over his future. In the end, he would be doomed to see more than he wanted, and the idea of having parts of their future relationship spoiled itched beneath his skin.

"Fianchra?" Quismat called. "I need the string glasses!"

The crow shifter huffed, ruffling his feathers in his roost amongst the shelves. "I don't think we have a pair anymore. Didn't Vasco borrow them when he left?"

Cursing, the god huffed, shaking his head. "Do you mind going to Lemminkainen for a pair?"

"As you wish, my lord," Fianchra proclaimed, flying off into the time stream.

He could have requested the same from Lemminkainen's mothers, but the younger god was more likely to provide the glasses without coming around to bother Quismat about his reasoning. Fianchra returned quickly enough, and putting on the glasses, the god of destiny cursed, shaking his head.

Strings were straightforward. The path to two fated mates or more finding one another wasn't always simple, but the strings themselves never lied. Whether thick and knotted or slim and smooth, strings were always red, and they held firm. Quismat's string was nothing like that. It buzzed, vibrating in and out of focus in a strange state of quantum flux. The string existed and did not exist simultaneously. Even if his mate were constantly teleporting, the string on his end should've appeared consistent.

Gods, like strings, had rules. All gods had mates. Eventually, all gods would meet said mate and consummate the bond or be rejected. There were almost no gods who found themselves permanently rejected, but the power settled in the mate's court by design. However, the rejection marred the string and weakened the god. If he were rejected, Quismat would know. Additionally, as he did not have a consummated mate bond, Quismat could not leave his realm. As the god never wanted to leave his realm anyway, it had never mattered, but with eons to accumulate power, he could astral project, and meditating, he sent himself forth to the mortal realm through the golden necklace he had given Kenji.

The wizard slept, sprawled on a cot in his work room. His equations suggested Kenji hadn't stopped his work. If he wasn't careful, Kenji would get himself killed. Frankly, if he were a god's mate, that was likely the only thing keeping the wizard sane if he had even temporarily fallen into the Nothingness.

Looking for the wizard's string, Quismat huffed as the strange flux was even worse on the wizard's end. The thread frayed, shimmering as if vibrating, and when Quismat's astral projection looked carefully, he couldn't be sure if the thread around Kenji's finger connected to his own. They both were mates and weren't.

Leaving the wizard, Quismat returned to his body, pacing the length of his room in the library before wandering down the maze of its halls. Like radiation poisoning, the Nothingness — if that was what it was — would leak through Kenji's consciousness, corrupting him from within until it broke down the wizard from the inside out.

Quismat took off the glasses, tucking them into his pocket. Kenji's life was worth more than his desire for surprise. Dropping the veil, Quismat looked into his future, but a sharp static shock sent him stumbling. He fumbled, smacking his head on a shelf before falling to the ground. Confused, he reached again. Another shock struck him down, sending the shelves around him scattering until the books floated, spinning about him in a mess before the shelves solidified, making order out of chaos once more.

"No-no-no," Quismat hissed, summoning his own book.

It was a vast volume — the largest in the collection, but when it arrived, it was as thin as Kenji's and petrified just the same. Something, or someone, had blocked his foresight. Two futures blurred together before him, but it was only the near future he could taste. In one, he and Kenji were fated mates, and in the other, Kenji had no fated mate at all.

"Rejection?" Quismat murmured.

As much as he believed that was the only possibility, the blurred near-future suggested nothing of the sort. Either Kenji was his mate and would be his mate, or Kenji had no red string. It was like nothing the god had seen or heard of before, and he had the entire wealth of the universe from beginning to end in his library.

Sitting on the floor with his book and Kenji's before him, Quismat reviewed every memory — every story — every last bit of information at his disposal, but nothing compared to this. He had nothing. No way to move forward. No way to ensure Kenji's future.

"What do I do?" Quismat asked the library as a whole, for the first time, he found himself loathing how empty his realm was. "If I don't know, none of the other gods would know. Unless I ask Lemminkainen...or his mother..."

Asking the goddess of love or her son seemed unlikely to help. Neither of them were known to be fond of complications or complaints regarding their realms. He had seen others find their lives immeasurably more unbearable after requesting aid from either of them, and while Lemminkainen had a better track record overall, half of that owed to the influence of his other mother and his shorter overall time as the god of love. The original gods, Quismat included, were known to be a bit more territorial, but that was hardly an excuse.

A great horned owl flew down, collapsing into a pile of feathers before Keren rose. Her brown hair fell around her chin in a short cut, and the wide circle of her goldene eyes stared straight through him.

"Are you ill, Lord Quismat?" the shifter asked.

Quismat shook his head, rising to his feet. "All is well, Keren. I'm simply being dramatic."

She didn't seem to believe him, but as he gathered his book, she shifted back to an owl and returned to her roost in a hollow of one of the stone walls.

The library had never faced disaster, and until he had answers, Quismat refused to worry those living in the library. He had sustained his realm without a mate, and if he needed to, Quismat would keep his realm stable for the rest of time.

Chapter Six

Before Kenji left home, his mother gave him a maneki-neko. The little gold cat with one paw lifted served as a lucky charm, and perhaps if he were a better son, he would have used it as a reminder to call home more than once a semester, but as much as he cared for his parents, they were both more involved in their work than in him and vice versa.

Which meant that when he needed something else to use to test his spellwork, Kenji turned to the maneki-neko. He duplicated it, watching as a single one turned into a dozen. Then he numbered them one through eleven. In each, he wrote little notes for Quismat. While he never believed he had a romantic bone in his body, his infatuation poured out. He complimented the god's calm disposition. Being with Quismat was a balm for Kenji's soul, and he drew little drawings, telling jokes in hopes of surprising the white-haired man. If they ended up in Quismat's library, that would be great, and if they didn't, well — then he'd have data for his hypothesis.

He then set them into the circle one after another. Each number coordinated with the amount of time he sent them forward into the future, and once they were sent, he waited, counting down for the first to arrive back. When it didn't, Kenji turned to summon the first one back.

Summoning the cat charm didn't go as planned. The second the spell completed, chaos exploded, sending Kenji flying against the wall of his workroom. His head smashed onto the stone, and as he slumped, that same darkness twisted — spreading emptiness before his eyes before shifting back to the workroom. A smoldering wreckage sat in the center of the summoning circle. Standing, the wizard stumbled. Spots danced in his vision, and he felt lifted out of his body before settling on the melted ruin of the cat charm.

"Fuck," Kenji groaned.

His entire body ached. As he scrambled to come up with a good enough excuse for the healing wing, a knocking resounded, leaving him to sink into a low crouch. A door appeared, and as it opened, Kenji vomited onto the mess of his workroom.

Quismat's calm voice called, "Kenji?"

Holding up a single finger, Kenji breathed out slowly. "I know you can't leave your realm since you're not mated, but — uhh, I could use a little help here."

Magic swept around the room, putting everything back to order, and it gently lifted Kenji, guiding him into the library, and as the door shut behind them, Quismat lifted Kenji with ease.

49

"Oh, wow," Kenji said, wrapping his arms around Quismat's neck. "This is doing it for me. The second there's only one of you, I'm going to shock myself on your dick."

Chuckling, Quismat smiled. "Sleep."

"Are you being nice to me before you scold me?" the wizard asked as the god set him into bed.

Sighing, the white-haired man shook his head. "I think you ended up scolding yourself enough."

"Hmm…my mouth tastes bad."

A wash of magic passed over him, leaving his mouth minty fresh. Humming happily, the wizard curled up, falling asleep as he pressed his face into the god's pillow, reveling in the scent of parchment and black tea.

When Kenji woke, his head felt better, but the scent remained around him, sheltering him in the warm softness of the god's bed. He rolled over, reaching out and knowing his hand would find the god without having to even look. It reminded him of the tea cup. Quismat had reached, believing his hand would find it, and Kenji moved the cup, so he did. Now, Kenji reached out, and Quismat shifted closer, allowing the wizard's hand to come and rest upon his own.

"Sleep," the god encouraged. "Time moves as fast or slow here as you need it to. You can always return exactly when you came."

50

Shimmying across the sheets, Kenji wrapped his arms around the god's waist, hanging half off the bed. "You should come to bed too."

"I don't need to sleep."

"Then lend me your lap," the wizard retorted.

With a sigh, the god pulled back, but Kenji held tight until Quismat huffed, "If you're well enough to argue, you're well enough to go back."

"But my head still hurts," Kenji whined playfully, smirking as he opened one eye to look at the god before him. "Come on, you know you want to…"

He expected some further argument, but the god climbed into the bed, sitting on his heels and letting the wizard wriggle into position. The softness of his thighs was cool beneath Kenji's head, and he sank back down into sleep as Quismat ran his fingers through the wizard's dark hair. When he woke again, the god still held him gently.

"You need to stop messing with the timeline," Quismat warned the wizard.

Kenji huffed. "It was just a little accident."

"Ten cat charms," the god grumbled, unpeeling Kenji's arms from around his waist despite the wizard complaining.

"Technically eleven, but I got one back," Kenji claimed as the god lined up the rest on the table. Unlike the one he summoned, these were all

51

still in relatively good shape. "Of course, that one melted, but I think that was an issue with my summoning circle."

"That was an issue with your head," Quismat retorted, setting his hands on his hips. "And number five is missing."

"Five? Just five?" Kenji sat up.

"And the one you summoned," the god replied, shaking his head. "I don't think you understand how dangerous the Nothingness is."

Waving his hand, the wizard clucked his tongue. "It's fine. They all found their way to you."

"Kenji..."

"I'm more curious about the five minute one. That's the same time span that I used when traveling physically, and I arrived in Amber's work room, so I thought it would just end up there since I ended up using the same spellwork," the wizard informed the god, reviewing the state of each charm. "All in all, they look in decent shape. Better than the snowy owl."

"The owl is a stuffed animal. It's not as durable," Quismat reminded Kenji.

Pulling out his pocket notebook, Kenji hummed softly, "I calculated reentry into the equation, but they all ended up in the Nothingness, right? That would explain why the summoning blew up. Maybe I can summon back the five minute one.

If it worked like my own, then it should've reentered the timestream. No harm done, right?"

"That's not exactly workable."

"Harm was done," Quismat protested, and when he slammed a large block of wood down on the table, Kenji frowned until it hit him.

Jaw dropping, Kenji gasped, "Is that your book?"

"Yes, and it should be larger and not a single wooden block!" the god proclaimed, shaking it before tossing it to join Kenji's own petrified book which was on the table.

Leaping to his feet, Kenji paced. "Do you realize what this means? This is the evidence I was looking for?"

"Evidence?"

"To disprove closed loop theory!" the wizard cheerfully exclaimed. He grinned, pulling Quismat to his feet. "I changed time!"

"This place is the hub of the time stream. Everything that is, was, and ever will be occurs at once in connection to here, and the only alteration is my personal — and linear, mind you — timeline," Quismat argued, pulling away from the wizard. "The exception isn't you changing just any old timeline. This is mine."

Kenji tilted his head. "So? You're fine. I'm fine. Doesn't this just mean you will have more surprises awaiting you? I thought you liked surprises."

"Not when they could kill you."

Immediately, the smile vanished from Kenji's face. "Not having a book could kill you?" He leapt to pick up Quismat's book. "How do I — there has to be a way to fix this."

"Nothing like this has happened before. I don't even know what this means, but our two books are the only ones affected. Even if I wanted to, I can't see along your or my timeline. Our connection is in a state of flux which no one could explain," Quismat explained, and the panic in his eyes went straight through Kenji, leaving a chill in his core. "I am the source of chaos in the time stream. Nothingness is the well, but my realm is the bucket. You are in flux, and it isn't even the flux of acceptance or rejection of a mate. It is mate or nothingness."

"Mate or — " The wizard's expression brightened. "I'm your mate."

Pulling at his white hair, the god groaned, "Yes and no. You are neither and both."

Kenji laughed. "I'm Schrodinger's mate."

"It's not funny, Kenji."

"It's a little bit funny."

Shaking his head, Quismat scoffed, "The longer you stay in flux, the more dangerous it will become."

"What are you saying?" Before the god could reply, Kenji rambled onward, "If I'm both your mate and not your mate, then I can't exactly accept or reject you because at any time I am influx, and if I accept, then I'm a god like you which means that I become the fifth person who can mess with time, right?"

"Second. Myself, my mate, Kon, and their mate," Quismat corrected.

"Kon?"

Sighing, the god sat back upon the bed. "Nothingness is a realm. The oldest god lives there. Their name is Kon."

"If anybody who went to the Nothingness and isn't a god would go insane, then his mate must be a god, and if the Nothingness is outside of time, shouldn't he already have his mate and both be in a state of always having had one?" Kenji posited before shaking his head. "But if I agree to become your mate, I become an exception that proves the rule, so any data I obtain is moot."

Quismat frowned. "By that argument, you should reject me."

Even the suggestion had Kenji's stomach twisting. If he rejected Quismat, then the god wouldn't have a mate, yet at the same time, while there was no record of god's getting second chances, Kenji pondered if Quismat might be an exception to that rule in the way he was an exception to the time stream. Anyone else being with Quismate struck the wizard as unacceptable, so he refused to open himself to that, yet at the same time, he couldn't reject the other man. Even if he did reject or accept, the conflict of being both a mate and not didn't necessarily fall into the rejection/acceptance conundrum. The way Quismat explained the matter left the wizard stunned. He both was and wasn't — even a rejected mate was still a mate. The bond still anchored the god, so it should've remained a solid state.

"I'm not doing that."

"Not accepting me? Or not rejecting me?" Quismat questioned, and Kenji just shook his head. "Kenji — if you don't make a decision, you could be in serious danger. We both could be."

"Could be. It's all uncertain now, right?" Kenji retorted.

He didn't give Quismat a chance to retort, pulling the god close, he kissed him, ignoring the burning sensation of the shock between their lips. Just touching Quismat sent his heart racing. If he were a being in flux and had dragged the white-haired god alongside him into the mire, then Kenji would take advantage of the nebulousness for as long as he could. Disproving closed loop time became a matter of urgency. In doing so, he would open up not just a world of infinite possibilities but free gods from their limitations of matehood. It was horrifying. It was electrifying. If he were Quismat's mate in the primary loop, then Kenji had no doubt he would regret this, but if he weren't — if by some fluke he became a potential mate by disproving closed loop time, then his very life depended on him continuing his research. Either way, he had no intention of giving Quismat up.

"I can't make a choice. Not now. Not yet," Kenji proclaimed. "I need to go back."

Stunned, the god summoned a door, and hardening his heart, Kenji crossed through it without looking back.

Chapter Seven

Though Quismat admired the younger man's tenacity, this was madness. His enthusiasm appealed to the god. As much as Quismat enjoyed the quiet calm of his library, the excitement which Kenji brought left him hungry for ore. He sought more. Craving the unexpected which poured out of the wizard with every meeting, Quismat lost himself to the rush, but he would not allow himself to indulge if it risked Kenji's life. The man deserved more. Mate or not, Kenji being alive came first.

No god had ever cut their cord, and he couldn't afford to do so without considering how that might affect more realms than he might endeavor to hope to count. Destiny and Death — they were not things to be taken lightly, and he could not force another to guard his realm. It was a calling. Being the only god to dip his feet into the Nothingness without coming back discolored for the journey, Quismat could not harm another in hopes of protecting himself. Not like the Goddess Below had done Enki, but with every passing moment, he feared disaster lurked. For Kenji, he might be more capable of underhanded cruelty than he dared believe.

Cutting the cord would be safest. If he undid the bond, any potential between them would evaporate, leaving nothing in flux. Nothing in question. Of course,the universe could also tremble — falling into chaos if he left a doorway open. Quismat dreamed of the beginning. That time before gods when heat boiled upside, and he woke in the dark. Nothingness stretched, and from the depth of it, something more came.

For the shortest moment, there were simply the two of them. Kon existed before. They treated Quismat like a child, pulling him close before the rest awoke and whispering secrets in his ear. While others forgot about Kon — for that is how they preferred it, Quismat remembered them.

Projecting himself into the Nothingness, Quismat searched the vast with dread emptiness. There was a single golden cat somewhere in the dark, and Quismat intended to find why he had not come across it before. Perhaps he would find Kon and speak with them about it.

When he came across a golden cat, he smiled, but the number upon it proclaimed it the fifty-seventh. One by one, Quismat found them in the vast, sending them back along his astral projection to the library through pockets in between. There were hundreds.

"That blasted fool," Quismat cursed.

He couldn't help the smile that twisted about his lips. If he could say nothing else about Kenji, the man had no idea when to give up.

"There are too many," a deep voice complained, and rippling across the dark, Kon's bright eyes stared out at Quismat.

Quismat offered a gentle smile. "Apologies, Kon. Kenji doesn't know when to give up."

"Hm."

"He seems to think that he can escape the time stream without consequence. He's absolutely brilliant," Quismat told the older being, but he sensed no amusement from Kon. Instead, he felt mounting frustration.

Shifting and forming in the pulsating emptiness, Kon released a tired sigh. "Your mate?"

"Perhaps. Maybe. It's complicated."

"Nothing is complicated. Love is transitory," Kon replied.

Quismat tumbled through the Nothingness. Pulled forward by Kon's will, he found himself drawn like a child being guided across the ocean's surface by its parent. The other brought him deeper and deeper into the void. Though there was nothing particularly solid within the void and little diverged from the rest with even Kon themselves blending into the background of this otherworldly place.

"Kenji believes he can change time. That rather than a single course, it may be diverted," Quismat struggled to explain. "I worry he'll end up hurt. He's in a strange state."

Kon hummed softly. "Is he?"

"Yes. In a flux of sorts. He exists, but his book turned to wood," the white-haired god proclaimed. "Mine too!"

"Ah, that does sound distressing."

It was so easy to relax in Kon's embrace, and as they drifted in the emptiness of chaos, Quismat lamented, "I'm afraid for him."

"Have no fear," Kon assured him. "Anything that slips between the cracks shall have my protection. It wasn't my realm that harmed that toy bird. You must warn Fiachra to file his talons."

"I appreciate that."

"Yes, which is why I'm glad you've finally come to fetch them," Kon announced, and dread pooled in Quismat's stomach.

"Them?"

Whatever secrets the Nothingness and Kon held, Quismat had no hopes of preparing for the shock that awaited him. A thousand surprises — this wasn't one he imagined possible. Caught in stasis, people floated like in their graves.

"Two witches, five demons, some fae, and one wizard," Kon explained, and as they reached the wizard, Quismat's stomach churned. Dread built inside him. "Ah, don't tell me this is your wizard."

"When did he arrive?" Quismat questioned, reaching for Kenji.

Uncertainty rippled as Kon laughed. "How would I judge that? He wasn't here, and then he was."

"Fine. We shall see to the rest first. Perhaps keeping him frozen like this will give fate a chance to settle about him," Quismat grumbled, though he simply had no desire to wake up the young man and discover his mind already harmed. "I will return to the library and see if I can identify the rest."

"Most agreeable."

Returning to the library should have answered something, but the more he sought answers for those who ended up in Kon's care, the less he found. Portals gone awry. Summonings screwed up by blessings and holy grounds which sent what came up right back down. These mistakes might be explainable, and setting the bulk back on course proved easy; however, finding empty slots only further assured Quismat that all of Kenji's theories were ridiculous. They came and went, people missing from their time, and the course of time moved on expecting them to return right back to it the moment he located and placed them. All those who came after the replacement showed signs of their time in the Nothingness, but it wasn't anything like Kenji. It only made him more and more concerned.

"Fiachra, there has to be a mistake," Quismat murmured, frowning.

The raven shifter hummed from the shelves, searching for the book in question. For some reason, the last demon's book proved impossible to find.

"Maybe the demon is like your wizard," the shifter proposed.

Quismat clucked his tongue. "If it were, I'd find him all the easier because the demon's book would be wood."

"Well, I can't find it," Fiachra proclaimed, sliding back down to land beside the god. "Perhaps one of the others will have had luck."

Huffing, the white-haired man shook his head. "No. It would be here. It must be here."

"How much do you know about that demon? Isn't it better just to toss him back the same way he came in?" the shifter asked, pulling his feet beneath him as he wrapped a blanket around himself. "Also, Branwen checked on Kenji, and he continues his experiments."

"That simply means we returned to the appropriate place in the timeline," Quismat retorted.

Humming, the shifter continued on his way, and Quismat focused on what he could, ignoring the rest. Limitations, however, forced him back, knocking aside the fruitlessness of his search as he returned to the Nothingness where Kon eagerly awaited.

"Your wizard has an obsession with cats," Kon complained, gathering the golden charms.

"I still can't seem to find the demon's source, and I can't tell where in the time stream this Kenji Nakamura came from," Quismat admitted. It put him ill at ease to see the man he adored standing so unnaturally still.

Kon hummed, and it reverberated along the whole of the emptiness. Before Quismat made any sense of what that sound meant, a flash broke through the void followed by a great shadow that had no place in the emptiness. When the Nothingness settled, a cry broke out, and a second Kenji — or perhaps a third — floated in the Nothingness.

"Quismat?" this other version beckoned, and then he fainted back into the dark, caught in Kon's embrace to slip alongside the first.

"Your wizard is troublesome," the great entity proclaimed.

"You can't just knock him out," Quismat cried, and wrapping his arms around the man, he drew Kenji close, but though they touched, the wizard felt eons away. "I'll bring him to the library. Both of them."

"Why are there even two of them?" Kon huffed, and before the god of destiny might open a door, Kon altered the Nothingness into an illusion of something. "Wake them here first. Reason yourself away."

Quismat's jaw dropped, but convincing Kon to change their mind proved impossible. When Kenji awoke with a start, Quismat's stomach churned.

"Kenji, please, look at me," Quismat begged. "You are in the Nothingness."

"The Nothingness?" Kenji repeated.

"It's outside of time. Outside of space."

"Outside — outside of space?" Laughing, the wizard ducked his head with a groan. "Then why am I seeing another me?"

"Because you are an idiot who fooled with powers beyond your understanding," Kon scolded, startling the wizard.

"Where did that — who was that?" Kenji proclaimed, turning only to find himself endlessly spinning until Quismat caught him in his arms. "I think I'm going to be sick…"

"That is Kon. Kon is the oldest of us, and you must focus," Quismat commanded.

Closing his eyes, the wizard nodded, struggling as he murmured about closed loops and ribbons. "All this — all this — and it's all the same."

"Kenji…"

Reaching out, his hand moved toward the other version of himself, and tension rippled through Kon, but the other did not speak — did not react as if testing a theory of their own. When

Kenji's hand brushed against the other Kenji, the two shifted. They were like a binary star system, but the weight proved unequal, and they collided together, swirling until only one remained in the vastness of who they were.

"Quismat?" this now singular Kenji called in confusion. "What is happening?"

"You were fragmented. Now, you are not," Kon explained lightly, humming as their attention shifted. "The demon has a duplicate which continues on. It felt the same. It is not a mate."

Kenji blanched. "A what?"

"Focus," Quismat begged.

"Does the Nothingness have a mate?" Kenji questioned, staring out as if his eyes might adjust to see Kon.

"Of course," Quismat huffed. "Kon is a god. All gods have mates."

Humming softly, Kon stretched across his realm like oil over water. "I am older than the gods. Older than all of you. My mate exists, but they are...sleeping." A soft brush like fingers over his face, comforted Quismat. "I know the pain of being forced to wait, little one."

"Little one?" Kenji laughed.

As if to mock them another Kenji appeared, sputtering in confusion, and Quismat cursed that the other man were a fool; however, as the pair — both awake — faced each other, and laughing all the while, Kenji reached out to greet himself, but as smoothly as the two looped together before, they did not do the same this time. An explosion like the first rippled across the Nothingness, and Quismat could not endure. The wave threw him back to the library, coming fumbling into his own body, and the moment he rose — determined to return — but it brought him down to his knees as blackness took him under.

Chapter Eight

Groaning, Kenji stormed his way through the castle, returning to his workshop after another mishap. He might've gotten a bit desperate. The second spell on himself wasn't easy, and he ended up back in Amber's workroom, but she wasn't there, so it was fine. Five minutes forward, fifteen minutes back. Ten minutes forward, two minutes back. A day ahead, an hour behind, and he was always just far enough out of reach that he couldn't reach himself as he was until it was too late. No further proof arose. All his data spilled out, and honestly, he lost more maneki-neko than he cared to admit.

"Why couldn't they install elevators in Aelion Academy? Did they think it would ruin the aesthetic?" the wizard complained, dragging himself up the stairs.

Aelion Academy acted like it was keeping tradition safe, but it was just a throwback aesthetic that left Kenji exhausted. He just wanted an elevator. Hell, he'd be happy with one of those stair chairs that old people could get. His entire body ached. A list of complaints rolled around in his head, but Kenji kept them to himself. He had bigger fish to fry than a college full of wizards who couldn't handle mortal technology.

Of course, he expected Quismat to appear to scold him, so he was rather shocked when he managed to go some time without hearing from the god. He had cursed more than once, debating with dread whether the other man had intended to ignore him after he refused to make a decision regarding the potential bond between them. It wasn't unreasonable. More and more, Kenji debated his own reasons, but he was mercurial on his best days.

Frustrated and tired, Kenji grew impatient. With himself. With the exhaustion which weighed his body down and the repeated failures. As if determined to examine the wreckage of himself, he set the gold door in the center of the mess of his room, tapping upon it with his finger. Though the knock must have resounded, he heard nothing in response.

"Oh, you know just how to pique my curiosity," the wizard laughed, and carefully, he opened the tiny door, longing to see into the miniature halls of the library.

To his surprise, a doorway fell in the center opening to him and beckoning him inside. With a shout of joy, he skipped along, wondering what wonders awaited him. He yearned to be pampered. To enjoy the fruits of the god's domain. They would flirt across the table from each other, and he'd make a move — anything to just look into those dark eyes and see the small smile play about Quismat's lips.

Maybe he would arrive just in time for tea. Quismat would be consumed with a book as he reached out across the table. Kenji would move his tea cup, just enjoying watching the god devour whatever literature he'd selected while enjoying a few sweets of his own until Quismat realized he'd arrived, and the startled flush would break into a pleased smile at being surprised again.

Wandering through the library, Kenji amused himself by reaching out to brush his fingers along the spines of books as he passed, debating plucking one from the shelf only to refuse in deference to Quismat. Temptation demanded, but if he intended to keep things uneven between himself and the god, he had every reason to hate the wizard, but he hoped desperately to be indulged. Not forever. Just a bit longer.

But why?

He could work his theories as an exception to the rule just as well as he could as a wizard. All of eternity might be dedicated if he allowed himself to have the man who he so desired. His heart yearned for Quismat. He dreamed of the god. In the fog between his work, he longed to be by the other man's side. To feel the softness of those plush lips and burrowing himself into the places where no one had ever touched before. To caress pale porcelain skin until it flushed. If he could leave his mark upon the god, then the beast beneath his breast might finally be fed.

Before he knew it, the wizard rushed, racing through the halls. His heart thundered in his chest. Whatever hesitation had held him back before, Kenji felt none of it now. All he could think about was Quismat. They should be together. Should have always been together, yet he wasted himself, wasted his time because of some idea of objectivity. He could prove them all wrong and have Quismat at his side. He had never denied himself much of anything, so why had he tormented himself and Quismat by denying them their happiness? It was as if doubts curled around him, twisting around him and pouring right off him.

As he turned into Quismat's room, Kenji smiled — grinning at the sight of the god sitting upon his bed. Pale lashes fluttered across his high cheeks. Everything Kenji wanted. Everything he feared to allow himself to have, and as Kenji reached forward to set a place alongside him — to rest his head upon the god's shoulder, Quismat sat up with a sharp cry. Those obsidian eyes sought for something, and as his gaze drifted across the library, they saw nothing. As quickly as he rose, he fell back upon the sheets.

"Quismat!" the wizard called, racing forward. He collected the god in his arms. "Quismat, what is happening?"

73

Panic swept him into its cold embrace. Kenji checked for a pulse, but his mind twisted in uncertainty. Did gods have pulses? Healing spells used to only matter as much as they could shape his own wounds after he proved too reckless. They came up empty. No reason explained. Just Quismat. Unconscious and in pain. Never had he felt more useless.

"Ah — you must be the wizard," a deep voice announced, and an obsidian figure stood. Like Quismat's inverse, the tall figure cut a terrifying shadow across the room. Looking at the figure straight on hurt. Bright lights burned from within their eyes. "Or — what's left of him."

It was like staring into a flickering light. The light burned his eyes, but he couldn't look away. Every hair on his body stood on end. Kenji could barely swallow. His blood ran cold.

"Who…?"

"I am Kon," the strange monstrous figure announced, and they did not walk. The world shifted around them. "And *you* have been too clever for your own good."

Kon took a step forward. Every survival instinct inside of Kenji screamed that this man should have never been here. That this thing didn't belong here.

"Whoever you are, keep your distance!" Kenji demanded, putting himself between the monster and Quismat. "Fucking back off!"

Kon frowned, tilting their head. "I have business with Quismat."

"You'll have to go through me!" Kenji growled, pulling up every bit of defensive magic he knew. The well of his magic ran dry, but desperation seemed to energize him. Chaos poured into him as if he had jumped right into the well itself. "Stay back!"

Laughter from the doorway pulled both their attention, and the wizard paled to see himself standing before him. The other him grinned, and deja vu echoed in Kenji's mind. In that moment, he could see himself from both sides. The him at the door — the him at Quismat's side. They were the same and separate. He tormented himself with the division.

"We have to close the loop, so to speak," Kon announced, humming in a way that made everything else vibrate along with them.

"It's simple. I've already done it twice," the other version of him said. "Come on. We need to get back to Aelion — leave this god nonsense behind."

Kenji's brows furrowed. "God nonsense?"

"Meeting Quismat was exciting, but we've never cared about gods. We have a hypothesis to support and a theory to disprove," the other version of him proclaimed. He swept into the room with a broad grin that looked so unfamiliar despite Kenji having seen it so often in the mirror and in photographs. "Come on! We don't want to be involved in this."

Kenji scoffed, shaking his head in disbelief. "I love Quismat. I'm not going anywhere."

"What? We don't have a mate," the other him stated.

"I love him," Kenji repeated. His fingers curled into fists, and clenching them, he growled, "I have no intention of walking away from this."

Clucking his tongue, the other shook his head. "Fine. Let's see. If we decide to become Quismat's mate, then we can move along the timeline with ease, right? This would be a closed loop, so if the mated version comes to arrive in thirty seconds, then we shall go through with the mating. Otherwise, we don't."

Kon groaned, "This is a fruitless endeavor."

Neither of the Kenjis paid him any mind. They counted down, waiting, but no version appeared. Holding out his hands, the other side of him laughed.

"There's your proof," the other version of him said, and he reached out his hand. "Come on. Let's finish this."

Clinging to Quimat, Kenji shook his head. "There's an explanation. A reason. I love Quismat."

"I have no intention of being influx for the rest of my life. Stop being so stupid, Kenji. We don't want this," the other shouted, moving closer.

Nothing of this made sense. Whatever this other version of himself thought, Kenji had no intention of leaving Quismat. Kon terrified him. Like some sort of Eldritch Horror, his existence twisted the world around him, scratching along his nerves. With the other version of him approaching, Kenji moved on instinct.

Throwing up a shield, Kenji pulled Quismat against his chest. Portals wouldn't work. He knew himself, and the library wasn't stable enough to allow him to portal from one place to another, so only one escape came to mind. Runes sprawled, burning into the wood floor, and the monster which had stayed back moved forward.

Kon's eyes dropped. Studying the runes, they called out, "Don't — "

Casting the same horomancy spell, Kenji ignored the horror's warnings, and in a flash of light, an explosion rippled through the library. Books went flying. Papers ripped. Spines broke, and emptiness stretched, but Kenji clung to Quismat, holding the god protectively to his chest. Wherever the dust settled, he and Quismat would be together. He just needed some more time.

Chapter Nine

Quismat woke with a pounding headache. Every swallow left pinpricks running down his throat, but he nuzzled into the warmth and familiar smell of ozone and chaos. Humming happily despite his pain, the god hugged the man who held him all the tighter.

"Kenji?" he murmured.

The arms around him held him tighter, squeezing the white-haired man as he opened his eyes. "Thank fuck," the wizard proclaimed, and as Quismat opened his eyes, lips pressed against his own.

It was nothing like before. Instead of the harsh spark when burnt his lips, the kiss sent a shiver through his body. Every nerve sprung to life with pleasure, and Quismat melted, opening his mouth to deepen the kiss as desire tightened in his belly. This was how a mating bond should feel. Everything settled in his chest, and without thinking, Quismat held tightly, dragging his fingers through the wizard's dark hair as fingers found their way beneath his shirt to press against his smooth, pale skin. Every touch drove Quismat mad with desire. He ached to feel those fingers painting patterns into his skin as pleasure tied them together.

"Don't ever freak me out like that again," Kenji commanded between kisses as he pressed the god down against the wood floor of the library.

Quismat moaned, spreading his legs to make room for the other man. His body yearned. Potential built up between them. A hollow of warmth bloomed in his core, and his cock rose in acknowledgement. All he wanted clung to him just as desperately as he clung to Kenji, and as their hearts thundered as one, the god allowed the rest of the world to drift away. None of it mattered. Kenji kissed him — touched him — loved him.

"Kenji!" the god exclaimed, breaking their kiss as his mind caught up with him. "Kon should've arrived. You fractured yourself in your time travel attempts — you need to — "

Before he could finish, the wizard pinned him down, swallowing his protests. Their tongues entwined, and all fight left Quismat. He wanted Kenji. Wanted to feel his yearning. To know that the bond between them stood stable, and every touch reassured him of this. Where it had fluctuated and caused them pain before, the red string remained stable — a promising hanging in the air between them.

"It's fine," Kenji reassured him. "It's done. I want you. I love you."

Smiling, the god pulled his mate closer. "I love you too."

It was easy to forget everything else — to hold onto Kenji and ignore the rest of the world aside, but the coldness of the floor left the library spinning around them. Books floating in the air, but none of it mattered.

"I should've never denied us," Kenji whispered, tugging the god's shirt off and tossing it aside as those clever fingers focused on undoing his trousers. "I should have consummated our bond the first time you mentioned it."

Quismat's brows furrowed. "If we're going to consummate, shouldn't we go to my room?" He frowned, moving to sit up, but Kenji pushed him back down, taking one of Quismat's pale nipples between his teeth as the wizard cupped the god's hardening manhood. "Kenji — we should do this in bed!"

"There was an explosion. Right here is fine," the wizard insisted.

His dark eyes sparkled, almost as swallowed by his pupil as Quismat's own black gaze. Every touch burned, pointedly demanding more, and the god had every intention of giving the wizard all that he had. Their bond thrummed, bright red between them. WIth each pulse, desire went straight to the god's cock, and as Kenji slipped between his sprawled legs, Quismat gasped in wonder. He never knew the heat of another's mouth around him, and the delighted slurp as Kenji licked at the head only further served to leave the god desperate and restless.

Methodical — determined and calculating in his every move, Kenji suckled before swallowing him to the root. Up and down, the wizard bobbed, taking him deeper until his nose pressed into soft white hair at the root of the god's manhood before backing away to lick and nuzzle along the shaft as fingers toyed with his balls, pressing back and behind to run across smooth skin. Back and forth, Kenji's fingers pressed and teased, circling but not pressing inside even as Quismat's fingers knotted in the other man's black hair.

Melted and completely at Kenji's mercy, the god could only keen and cry in pleasure, desperate as air escaped him. His entire realm shifted, a mess and swirl of potentials — of futures and pasts — that twisted outside his grip. He anchored himself to Kenji. He needed nothing else. Wanted nothing else. The warm wetness of the wizard's mouth and throat, his clever tongue toying until Quismat's legs quaked — it overwhelmed a man unused to surprise. Unaccustomed to the burning desperation which left him arching off the unforgiving wooden floor to come down the other man's throat.

But it wasn't enough. Fingers rubbed, tracing circles until wetness throbbed, dripping slick from his core. His entire body submitted, welcoming his mate closer. If his heart beat any faster, it would free itself from the cage of his ribs.

Flipped upon his stomach, Quismat cried out, not expecting the tongue that had teased his cock to spear him as those teasing fingers spread his cheeks and left him all the more at Kenji's mercy. Their bond ached to be fulfilled. Crying out, Quismat bit his knuckles, desperate to silence the uncontrolled whimpers which left him flushed and trembling at the wizard ministrations.

"None of that," Kenji scolded, pulling Quismat's hand back to pin it to the dark wood floor. "I want to hear you."

Sobbing in shock as Kenji's cock ran between the valley of his cheeks, Quismat ground back, struggling to contain the multitudes which exploded beneath his skin. "Then fuck me already!"

"You're not ready," the wizard protested, and to accentuate his point, he thrust two fingers into the mess of Quismat's body, twisting and stretching them until tears lined the god's pale lashes like tiny diamonds. "First, I'm going to open you up. Then — I'm going to consummate our bond until you can't stand. Then when you think you can't come again, I'll prove you wrong."

Quismat moaned, clenching around the fingers inside him. Pink painted his pale skin. The heat in his entirely black eyes drove Kenji mad with longing, and his desire radiated through the air of

83

the library which thrummed in perfect harmony with the ever growing fires of their passion. With his tongue and fingers, the wizard took him apart, preparing the gods body until the slick wetness of him squelched, sending the lewdest of sounds through the air above their groans. When neither could bear being separated for a moment longer, Kenji aligned himself and drove his hips forward.

The head of his cock popped inside. Moaning, Kenji tossed his head back, driving deeper and deeper in careful thrusts. For every glide forward, he pushed just a bit more. All around them, the library spun. Books danced, and the chaos of the emptiness peeked through, but Kenji held firmly to Quismat's hips. His bruising grip only fed the flames of lust. They moved in unison, two beasts driving forward and falling back again until all sense left them. Their bond blazed. Gold and red flared, and the pair lost themselves in the current of their affection.

"I'll make a mess of you. Leave you wrecked until you think you can't take anymore, and then I'll have you again," Kenji whispered, his hot breath fanning against the god's ear. "I'll surprise you with how wanton you can be."

Quismat groaned, ducking his head, but he rolled his hips back, meeting every thrust the other gave. "Maybe I've always been a salacious slut."

"Oh, tell me about it," Kenji crooned.

"About what?"

Wrapping an arm around Quismat's chest, the wizard pulled him back, lifting him to drive his cock deeper into the clutch of the god's body. "Tell me about how salacious you are. Did you finger yourself thinking of me?"

"It might surprise you, but I didn't assume this was the way it would go between us. I fisted my cock to the scent of you in my bed, imagined reaching across the table to kiss you — dreamed of how sweet you would taste," the god purred, and when Kenji's fingers wrapped around him, Quismat moaned in relief.

When they came in unison, their bond solidified. An unbreakable golden string bound them. Now, Kenji was his mate, a god in his own right. Their powers shared and increased. The heat of his seed sloshed in Quismat's belly, and when his mate lifted him, the white-haired man gasped, clenching though Kenji obviously had no intention of slipping from the warmth of his body. Instead, Kenji settled him upon his lap, legs spread and the connection of their body obvious to any who might appear as Kenji settled against the shelves. Lips sucked livid marks in pale flesh. Arms like iron wrapped around Quismat, daring any to come and try to take him away. Those dark eyes promised to rend flesh from bone of any who tried.

However, Quismat hadn't expected anyone to come across them. The shifting shelves should've warned the shifters who lived in the library, and there were so few anyway amongst the endless halls and shelves, so he didn't expect Kon to appear with another version of Kenji beside him.

When Quismat moved to stand, his mate held fast, holding him firmly in place and growling like a beast over his shoulder. "You can't take him from me."

"That was never my intention," Kon retorted calmly.

However, the other Kenji — the one still mortal and a wizard — frowned. "It's like looking at a completely different person. Can we even still unify?"

"No. He's effectively cut himself off from you," Kon informed the other version. "You will need to go back. You are now Kenji Nakamura — wizard."

Holding firmly to Quismat, the Kenji who was his mate huffed, "That works for me. I have everything I want right here."

"Kenji, you said — " the white-haired god trailed off, shaking his head. "No, that was my error. I assumed...but why?"

"I love you," his mate professed, and he could feel the truth of it through their bond. "He intended for us not to be together. I couldn't — I couldn't do that. I love you. I refuse to let anyone — even myself — take you from me." Glaring at the other version of himself, Kenji held his head up high. "You're an idiot for not wanting this."

Quismat ducked his head, cheeks heating, and to his greater embarrassment, he clenched, feeling Kenji's cock hardening slowly within him. Covering himself with his hands, the god summoned a blanket, wrapping it around themselves despite the huff of disappointment from his mate.

"That's fine. This was always meant to be," Kon proclaimed, brushing the stress aside as he smiled. "Open a door and put this other one back. It does mean — god-Kenji — that you may never return to a time when wizard-Kenji exists."

Grinning, Quismat's mate laughed. "That leaves eons to explore."

"It also explains why the mate version of you didn't go back in time. Hm, perhaps time is a closed loop," the wizard hummed, muttering in consideration as he studied the scene before him.

It was strange to sit across from the man who was identical in looks to his mate and see no interest in the other's eyes, but Quismat found he felt much the same. The man before him wasn't Kenji — despite the name they shared, and the man behind him held him firm, leaving it easy to separate the two in his mind.

The world shifted, and Kon pressed a kiss to Quismat's brow. "Congratulations."

"Thank you, Kon."

"I have a demon to deal with, little one. After you are settled, come find me. Bring your mate if you desire. He should be better suited to the void now that your bond is consummated," the oldest of all gods proclaimed before melting back into the Nothingness.

"Even as a god, I still don't like them," Kenji muttered into Quismat's shoulder once the other vanished.

With a snap of his fingers, a doorway opened, and the wizard-Kenji left back to his workshop without another glance at them. He would set aside time travel, focusing on other applications and theories. His future would ensure their paths never crossed again as he accepted the reality placed before him and the limitations of his magic.

"You do realize you'll never see your friends and family again. The duration of that Kenji's life will be out of reach for you — even as a god, you have limits," Quismat told his mate as he leaned back into the other man's warm chest. "I had never wanted you to give up so much for me."

Kenji laughed, hugging him tightly. "It isn't much. I've never been sentimental, and honestly, escaping the expectations my parents had is well worth the exchange."

"What about your friends?"

"My life was my research, Quismat. I didn't have friends," Kenji easily admitted. "Now, what say we find a bed? We can talk more after I've kept my promise."

Quismat stood, stepping forward only to flush as his mate's seed oozed from his hole. He blushed, reaching behind to see Kenji watching with rapt interest. Biting his lip, the white-haired god spread his legs, spreading his cheeks to show off his entrance.

"You made a mess," the white-haired god scolded teasingly.

Smirking, Kenji reached out, but the older man danced out of reach. "Come back here. You can't show such a tempting sight and expect me not to take you right here and now."

"What? Can't you catch me?" Quismat taunted.

Kenji lunged, but the god danced ahead. Naked and glowing, Quismat ran, laughing as his mate chased him through the halls.

Chapter Ten

If Quismat intended for them to talk, he would have been disappointed, but Kenji doubted the god was too upset by the turn of events. When they had come across a desk, Kenji realized how little of the library he had actually explored, and it would be a pity to walk by a desk and another nook with another bed without making use of both. This endless labyrinth likely had more. The former wizard intended to enjoy every single one.

Kenji couldn't get enough. His fingers pressed, delighting when bruises remained like shadows on that gorgeous pale skin. It was like the first snow of winter. He had the privilege of racing through it — marking it as his own, and every roll of Quismat's hips urged him to go faster, to press deeper. The other man ached for him. They wanted the same thing, and it was so easy to allow them both to have it after everything. Every load poured inside, joining the rest, and godly stamina allowed Kenji to just keep coming, just keep filling the man beneath him. Soon, it would take hold.

The image haunted him. A promise that he could almost taste. Quismat curled in an alcove with a good book. Cradled in a nest that Kenji could make, the other god would glow, cheeks painted pink and lips plush as his belly rounded. Their child would reshape him. What could be more spontaneous — more delightfully unpredictable than a child? The perfect combination of the two of them. All of Quismat's calm playfulness — all of Kenji's desperate and eager thirst for knowledge. They would make the most brilliant child. They would have a life, exploring together. The whole universe stood before them, and give or take a few hundred years around the other version of him, they had endless possibilities to explore. Eternity even.

Every pistoning of his hips drove his cock into the wet, warm mess he left behind. He filled the white-haired god until seed spilled out with every thrust. Loud wanton moans shifted to gasps and keens as Quismat trembled, growing weak beneath the constant onslaught of pleasure. He had never known touch like this. His own pleasure rarely drew his attention, but now, neither of them could get enough. Their bodies called to one another. The exploration beckoned Kenji.

If he brushed his fingers along Quismat's ribs, would he clench tighter? Would he let out a breathless gasp? When Kenji sank his teeth into soft skin, leaving an imprint, would the white-haired god come, spurting his own release beneath him? Bent in half, could Quismat's knees reach his ears? Could Kenji's cock press deeper until the weight of every load rounded the white-haired god's belly?

There were so many questions. So many unanswered questions and every time he discovered how Quismat might react, repeated study would lead to a surprise that left Kenji hungry for more. He would never have enough. Love burned in his chest. They had the whole universe to explore, and while he had never wanted anyone at his side before, Kenji couldn't imagine going forward without Quismat at his side — without Quismat to return to. Who else would he discuss theory with? Who else's opinion did he actually care about in this wild bizarre universe?

"You've grown quiet," Kenji murmured as he rolled his hips, driving his cock deeper. "This isn't enough for you anymore, is it?"

Bent over his desk, Quismat moaned. Beautiful and piteous as tears like diamonds dotted his pale lashes. When Kenji oved to still, Quismat ground back, begging wordlessly for more despite the way his mate had already ruined him. Left him wet and sloppy and dripping. He would gap, leaking Kenji's spend if nothing plugged it, and wasn't that an appealing thought? Plugging Quismat up tight and keeping him wet and ready. He could nap in his dark blankets, purring as Kenji read to him until they couldn't stand being apart any longer. Their hips slapped with each thrust, leaving the white-haired man to cling to his desk as his cum-swollen belly swung with each drive of his mate's hips. Every thrust caused cum to leak out, but Kenji guided it right back inside until Quismat came with a sob, spraying his load onto the library's wooden floor as the shelves spun around them.

Kenji's hands roamed Quismat's back, massaging his pale ass. "You're sucking me dry. Let me look at you," the black-haired man groaned as his hands slid down to cup Quismat's bloated belly. The weight of it as his cum sloshed around inside the god's fertile form held promise. "Fuck, this shouldn't be possible."

"We're gods," Quismat reminded him.

As Kenji's cock slipped free, Quismat sagged forward, but his mate flipped him onto his back, pressing down on his bloated stomach and groaning at the flood of cum which gushed from the white-haired man's pink hole. A shuddering breath left Kenji's lips. He hated it and loved it. His seed belonged firmly inside Quismat, rounding his belly and reminding the white-haired god exactly how loved he was, but watching it pour from his well-used hole as Quismat sagged, panting as heat poured from his body enticed Kenji to fill him once more.

"I never thought this could be hot, but fuck…" Kenji groaned, shaking his head before he dove down between the white-haired man's legs. Kiss marks marred creamy thighs, and as Kenji sucked his seed which mixed with Quismat's slick, the black-haired man moaned. "Gonna make a nest.

Bundle you up and keep you full until it takes. Keep you caught on my cock."

Even his own seed which usually didn't appeal to him tasted sweeter for having been inside Quismat. He could eat him out, scrap his essence from the god's body only to fill him up once more. It would be so simple. A twist of his fingers — they could clean the mess with a thought. This was their realm now. It would shift as they desired.

Keening, Quismat tangled his fingers in Kenji's dark hair. "We should talk about what happened."

"Or I could eat you out," Kenji retorted, licking and nuzzling at the white-haired god's cock, he pouted. "What do you want me to say? That other version of me refused to see reason. You are mine. I am yours. I love you. That wasn't happening."

Quismat sighed. "I love you too."

"Then forget that other me. I'm here with you now. You're my mate," Kenji possessively proclaimed.

Sliding into the mess between Quismat's thighs, he fucked inside him once more. He twisted the white-haired god's nipples, grinning as Quismat's long legs wrapped around his waist, pulling Kenji closer. Their bodies moved together, chasing another peak.

"You realize this was a closed loop event," Quismat teased, only to cry out as Kenji sunk his teeth into his neck, leaving another mark in his wake.

Clucking his tongue, Kenji retorted, "We're gods of destiny — time bends itself to our will."

"Well, not exactly…"

"I'm going to prove my theory yet! The only reason this ended the way it did is because I wanted it to," Kenji claimed, and Quismat laughed until Kenji's determined thrusts left him unable to do anything but cling to his mate as the black-haired man added to the mess within his belly.

Lifting Quismat from the desk, Kenji carried him to bed, and they tumbled into the blankets together. Curled around each other, they held fast as if something might come and steal the other from them.

"Tell me you're not just going to spend your time trying to prove time isn't a closed loop," Quismat asked, cupping the younger's face in his hands.

Kenji laughed, lifting himself and tossing a leg over to straddle his mate. "Is that what you think of me?"

Tilting his head, Quismat frowned, considering before admitting, "You're fickle. Unpredictable." Before Kenji could even feign offense, the other added, "I like that."

96

Kenji reached his fingers behind him, driving them into Quismat and taking his own cum. He opened himself, swiveling his hips to drive their cocks together until they rose, hardening with every swivel of his hips. It was a show Quismat never expected. He had never looked into his future, longing for surprise, so he had not considered that their positions might shift — especially not so soon in the course of their lovemaking. His body trembled, unaccustomed and petrified that he might disappoint, but Kenji never gave him a chance.

"I'm a fan of spontaneity," Kenji proclaimed as he wrapped a hand around his mate's cock, guiding it inside himself. As he sunk down inch by inch, he offered an almost feral grin. "I came to the library because it was a new adventure, and the only reason I flirted the first moment I saw you. When I ran away, it was because of my own indecisiveness."

"If you weren't certain, then there was a reason. I don't want you to regret us," Quismat moaned, holding onto Kenji's hips as the other bounced in slow, methodical movements. Up and down, driving down with a cocky flush of his cheeks.

Kenji shook his head. "Those parts of me — I had to cut them. They weren't the me that belonged with you — that deserved you."

Quismat groaned, trembling as Kenji's warmth squeezed his cock, milking him. "Are you honestly jealous of yourself?"

"Yes. That idiot touched you and didn't take you the moment it was an option," Kenji growled, clenching his thighs about Quismat's hips. "They were the reason I hesitated. Closed loop, rewritten history — I don't care. As long as I can come home to you, that's all that matters to me. I love you."

Chest heavy, Quismat sobbed, "I love you too!"

Every time Kenji pressed down, taking him to the hilt, the pressure pushed more of the black-haired man's seed from Quismat's body, leaving his thighs all the wetter and stickier, reminding him of how deep his mate had filled him and how full. Everything inside his body rose, growing more and more until he couldn't contain the heat coiling tighter and tighter inside him. The tight heat of Kenji's body pulled him over the edge. Moaning, Quismat came. His seed flooded the younger's body, and before he could recover, Kenji slipped off him and bent Quismat in half to thrust inside him once more.

"Besides, if I didn't explore the edges of the universe, we'd both end up bored stiff! I'm going to light up your life, baby," Kenji promised.

When Quismat laughed, the black-haired man took his cock in hand, driving faster and faster into his mate's body as he jerked Quismat off in time with his thrusts. Laughter turned to moans. Kenji stole his mate's lips in a kiss. Beneath the sheets in the library, the two melted against one another.

"You know you could wind up pregnant too," Quismat reminded Kenji in the afterglow.

Humming softly, the dark-haired man considered the possibility. "Odds are in your favor, but it could happen."

"Another surprise?" the white-haired man chuckled.

Pressing a kiss to the white-haired god's cheek, Kenji made his way between Quismat's legs. "I suppose we'll just have to wait and see."

Their books were no longer wood. The future stood before them, but as it no longer hovered on the precipice of disaster, neither cared to look into the future. Whatever happened, they would face it together, and that was the true adventure.

Epilogue

Curled in an alcove, Quismat rested one hand upon the curve of his belly. They had expected that their first marathon of lovemaking would result in a child, and Kenji even joked that there might be twins or more by the time he was done, but as neither purposefully tried to conceive, fate left without for longer than either could have expected. They enjoyed their time together, exploring the limitations of the library. Everything which once seemed so straightforward and plain became magical in Kenji's eyes — though the black-haired man still disliked the Nothingness more than Quismat expected.

Now, however, their first born grew inside Quismat. Despite each taking turns, it seemed fate recognized Quismat the safer bet of the two. While Kenji often took trips out of the library, racing across history to collect information firsthand when he might have learned it from the texts, Quismat enjoyed those quiet times. They made him all the more eager to listen to his mate's stories when the other returned. Objective truths existed in the shelves of destiny, but hearing the stories colored by Kenji's thoughts always appealed to him more.

As their unborn child kicked, Quismat smiled, setting aside his book. "Thank you for the warning, little one."

Sure enough, as their child had predicted, a doorway appeared. Kenji trudged through in armor. Putting up the visor of his helm, the black-haired god grinned. "I've done it!"

"Done what?" Quismat asked.

"You see — there was this dark knight, and I read his book the other day not expecting I would come across him, but the idiot tried to rob me in the woods," Kenji announced as he slowly worked to undo his armor, getting caught as he seemed to forget his own powers. Then again, perhaps he just wanted to lure his mate close. When the white-haired man crossed to help him, he continued, "So I decided to intervene in the black knight's love life, unmasking him to his mate five years ahead of schedule, which changed everything!"

Humming, Quismat hid a smile. "Did it?"

Dropping the last off his armor, Kenji swept the clothes away, freshening up with the very magic he had just avoided using. "Don't you see? I proved time isn't a closed loop."

"My heart, you are a god of destiny. The library is an extension of your domain, and whenever one or both of us leave even temporarily, everything goes into flux," Quismat reminded him, and pulling the book of the knight in question, he flipped it open. "The book rewrote as well."

"Fuck."

"You aren't part of the timestream. Not anymore and not the same way. You can intervene. I've done it since the beginning, but that doesn't change things because — in some ways — you become entrapped in that aid," Quismat warned him, rubbing his back as their child shifted.

Seeing the strain in the white-haired god's dark eyes, Kenji knelt, pressing a kiss to the top of the other god's belly. "Are you giving your papa trouble?"

A forceful kick appeared to reply in the affirmative, and Kenji laughed, rising to pull Quismat into a kiss. There was nothing like a homecoming. They lost themselves in the softest of touches, simply reveling to feel the warmth of the other in their arms.

"Still, you remember it, and I remember it, so time can be rewritten," Kenji proclaimed with a slight pout.

Not wanting to upset his mate, Quismat set aside his hesitancy, humming in agreement. "Perhaps — though…"

"Though what?"

"I found a book about a mortal king and fae prince that you're in," Quismat noted, and handing the book to him, the white-haired god smiled. "And that isn't the only one."

"What if I don't go?" Kenji questioned, shoving the books aside. "We have all the time in the world — in the universe really."

Smiling, Quismat nodded. "We do."

"I could wait until the last minute and still make it in time. Besides, you aren't pregnant in that first one, and in the one with the sorcerer and the fae prince, I could always just send Fiachra to tell a stringmaster what they needed to know to prompt the queen to rush the meeting," Kenji argued as he pulled his mate into a simple box step. "And what if I don't want to help them at all? The books will rewrite themselves won't they?"

Brows furrowing, Quismat frowned. "But what if the mortal king goes forward with cutting the thread, and the sorcerer is so lonely."

Kenji groaned. "That pout is blackmail."

"The stringmaster also matches your description," Quismat noted, laughing at the glare his mate sent his way.

Cursing, Kenji shook his head. "I'm only doing this because you want me to. This is an act of love!"

"I had no doubt."

Pulling Quismat into a lurid kiss, Kenji allowed his hands to wander over his love's gravid form, moaning reluctantly as he stepped back. Both of them swayed, pulled closer by the gravity of their bond, but the dark-haired god put some distance between them, fighting the urge to simply take his mate to bed.

"I'll take care of that stringmaster business, and then I'm coming back here and having my way with you. You weren't pregnant in the mortal king one," Kenji announced, and gesturing toward the bed, he added, "You better be ready. This will be an afternoon for me, but I'll be back in an instant for you, and then I'm going to see if godly magic can turn our first born into twins."

Quismat smiled. "Maybe if you put your back into it."

"Ha ha — you think you're funny now, baby, but I'm going to strip you down and have you ride me until neither of us can stand it anymore," Kenji promised as he summoned another door and transformed his clothes into a fae style, placing a glamor about himself before slipping off to Faerie.

As much as Kenji might complain, the other man would undoubtedly delight in his cameos through history.

Returning to his nest of pillows and blankets, Quismat rubbed a hand over his belly, laughing. "Your father always keeps us on our toys, doesn't he?"

Sign up to the J.B. Black newsletter for a free M/M Erotic Romance Fantasy and monthly updates on upcoming sales!

Other Works By JB Black:

Nobility Fated Mates Novellas
The Fae King's Fated Mate
The Fae Prince's Fated Mate
The Fae Lord's Fated Mate
The Crown Prince's Fated Mate
The Sorcerer's Desert King
The Erlkonig's Fated Mate
The Warlock's Royal Admirer
The Warlock's Questing Prince
The Fae Prince's Unseelie King
The Warlock's Viking King
The Warlock's Royal Courtship
A Fae Prince for the Mortal King
The Warlock's Emperor

Fated Mates of Gods Novellas
The Wandering Warlock's Fated Mate
Forest God's Fertile Hunter
From Forest God's Head Scribe to Fertile Bride
The Island God's Fated Mate
The Sea God's Pirate Mate
Fated for the Harvest God
Claiming the God Below
Claiming the Sea God
Claimed by the Crossroad God

Fated Mate Box Sets
Psychics, Wizards, & Dragons

Fated Mates & Gods

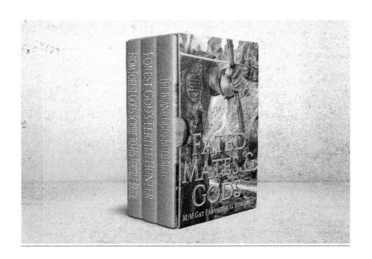

Royal Faes

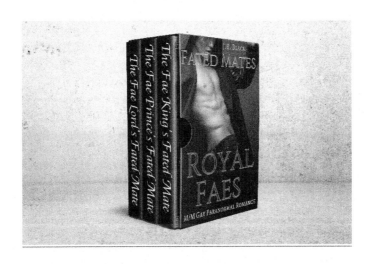

Warlock Mates

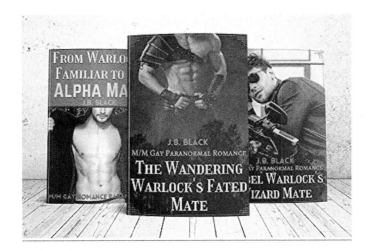

Bards, Dwarves, and Sirens

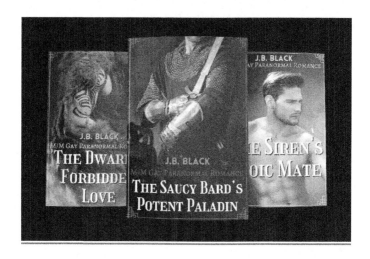

Bards, Dwarves, and Sirens

Printed in Great Britain
by Amazon

47698950R00069